The Queen of Hearts

By Dona Herweck Rice
Illustrated by Rayanne Vieira

Publishing Credits

Rachelle Cracchiolo, M.S.Ed., *Publisher*
Emily R. Smith, M.A.Ed., *VP of Content Development*
Véronique Bos, *Creative Director*
Dani Neiley, *Associate Editor*
Kevin Pham, *Graphic Designer*

Image Credits

Illustrated by Rayanne Vieira

Library of Congress Cataloging-in-Publication Data

Names: Rice, Dona, author. | Vieira, Rayanne, illustrator.
Title: The Queen of Hearts / by Dona Herweck Rice ; illustrated by
  Rayanne Vieira.
Description: Huntington Beach, CA : Teacher Created Materials,
  [2022] | Audience: Grades 2-3. | Summary: ""The Queen of Hearts
  remembers how much fun it is to bake tarts. But the Knave of
  Hearts can't keep from stealing them--they are so good! What's
  a queen to do?""-- Provided by publisher.
Identifiers: LCCN 2021051035 (print) | LCCN 2021051036 (ebook) |
  ISBN 9781087601830 (paperback) | ISBN 9781087631899 (ebook)
Subjects: LCSH: Readers (Primary) | LCGFT: Readers (Publications)
Classification: LCC PE1119.2 .R5368 2022 (print) | LCC PE1119.2
  (ebook) | DDC 428.6/2--dc23/eng/20211029
LC record available at https://lccn.loc.gov/2021051035
LC ebook record available at https://lccn.loc.gov/2021051036"

TCM | Teacher Created Materials

5482 Argosy Avenue
Huntington Beach, CA 92649
www.tcmpub.com

ISBN 978-1-0876-0183-0
© 2022 Teacher Created Materials, Inc.

Printed by 51250
PO 10851 / Printed in USA

Table of Contents

Chapter One

—◆—

The Queen of Hearts

Harriet was bored. Being queen should be great fun! But really, there was very little to do. The Kingdom of Hearts almost ran itself. Everywhere she went, there was just love, love, and more love. The twos loved the threes. The threes loved the eights. The eights loved the tens. And on and on it went. With so much love everywhere, the kingdom ran as smooth as silk. What was a queen to do?

5

6

"There's nothing for me to do in our kingdom anymore. Everyone is so happy," the queen complained to Harry, the king. "I need a hobby."

"Well, my dear, what do you like to do?" Harry replied.

The queen had a sudden memory. "When I was a little girl, I used to bake with my grandfather. He was a wonderful baker," she answered.

"That must have been delicious!" the king cried.

"It was!" the queen said, licking her lips at the thought.

"I think you found your answer, my dear," Harry said with a grin.

Chapter Two

She Made Some Tarts

Harriet shuffled to the palace kitchen. She was hoping to find her grandfather's recipe book there. It was tucked out of sight on a high shelf. *Tarts for Your Hearts* the book read. "Yum!" Harriet said.

Harriet flipped until she found the recipe for strawberry tarts. "I'll make these!" she declared. She grabbed all the ingredients she could find. She asked Ace, the youngest card in the deck, to pick strawberries for her from the palace garden.

Ace brought Harriet a heap of strawberries. Harriet got out a big mixing bowl, a wooden spoon, and a rolling pin. Then, she mixed and she rolled. She filled and she crimped. Finally, she placed the tarts in the oven to bake. Their sweet, fruity smell soon filled the castle.

The smell got the attention of every card in the deck. Before long, they were all shuffling along to see where the delicious smell was coming from. The fives sniffed the air. The sevens licked their lips. Jack, a knave, thought he had never smelled anything so good.

Chapter Three

He Stole the Tarts

When the tarts were finished baking, Harriet took them from the oven. She placed them on the window ledge to cool. All the cards were eager to have a taste. But it was all too much for Jack! He could not resist. He grabbed the tarts and ran off to hide among the diamonds. He wanted all the tarts for himself.

When Harriet returned for the cooled tarts, she found only an empty baking sheet. "Harry!" she cried. "Someone has taken my tarts!"

"Who could have done such a thing?" the king growled. "I will call all the deck at once!"

The royal joker blew a trumpet to call all the cards to the great hall. They all assembled. Harry asked them sternly, "Who has taken the queen's tarts?"

Everyone was silent. Queen Harriet and King Harry looked at them closely. There was no way to tell who had taken the tarts.

Or was there?

Chapter Four

And Vowed He'd Steal No More

The Knave of Hearts stood in line with all the others, strawberry jam smeared across his chin.

"Do you have something you wish to tell me?" Queen Harriet asked him, her eyes narrowed.

"Mmph mmph mmph," Jack mumbled. He was still chewing the last of the delicious tarts.

"Is it possible you took the tarts?" King Harry asked.

Jack swallowed. He knew he should answer truthfully. "Yes, sir, I did," Jack replied guiltily. "But they smelled so good! That is my only defense."

"Jack, this is the Kingdom of Hearts. We all love one another here. You only have to ask for what you want!" Queen Harriet said with a smile.

Jack hung his head shamefully. "I'm sorry, Queen Harriet. I should have asked. I'll never do it again!" Then, Jack had a thought. "Can I make some new tarts to replace the ones I ate?"

Harriet smiled and patted Jack on the back. "We'll make them together. We'll make them for everyone!"

The whole deck cheered. Then, Harriet and Jack got down to business, making tarts for all the hearts. And although Jack licked the bowl and was covered in strawberry jam, he never did steal a tart again.

About Us

The Author

Dona Herweck Rice is a former teacher, a theatre director, and a professional writer who lives and works in California. She also thinks she's a real card and even a joker. In fact, she thinks her jokes are aces. Her family may not always agree, but they think she's a diamond anyway and treat her like a queen. They suit Dona very well, and she's glad her deck is stacked with hearts. She's sure she has a winning hand!

The Illustrator

Rayanne Vieira lives in Brazil. She loves drawing characters to give them their own personalities. When she's not drawing, she's usually watching cartoons or reading comics.